ELLIOT AND THE RACCOONS' WILD PARTY

Copyright © 2020 by Ingrid Simunic, PhD. All rights reserved.

DSCVR Inc., *Keep Discovering*

Thank you to the Sag Harbor Cinema, The American Hotel, and BuddhaBerry for their permission and enthusiasm to be included in the story's illustrations. HarborFest is organized by the Sag Harbor Chamber of Commerce.

No part of this publication may be reproduced, stored in a retrieval system, or transmitted in any form or by any means, electronic, mechanical, photocopied, recorded, or otherwise, without written permission of the author.
Write to: info@dscvrinc.com

For a list of books in the Elliot's Adventures series, visit us online at www.elliotsadventures.com
Social media: @elliotseries

Hardcover: 978-1-7351023-6-8
Paperback: 978-1-7351023-7-5
Kindle: 978-1-7351023-8-2
ePub: 978-1-7351023-5-1

FIRST EDITION

To my sweet son and nephews, who are avid readers and helped shape the characters in this book.

On the eve of HarborFest, Elliot hosted his friends for two very important things: pizza and planning. Tomorrow, Sag Harbor would completely transform. There would be races, games, live music, and . . .

"Hot dogs!" Nico shouted.

"OMG, Nico. Do you ever stop thinking about food?" Layla said.

"Hey! I get hungry when I'm nervous," Nico said.

"OK, guys. Focus," Elliot said. "We know how to win the tug-of-war: arrange ourselves according to our diagram, and do it first, while we've got all our strength. But we still need to plan the three-legged race."

When they finally settled whether to pair up according to leg length or running speed (and convinced Nico that cotton candy should come *after* victory), they said goodbye.
"Sounds like you'd better get a good night's rest," Mom said.

"Take out the garbage, please, and then go to bed. And don't forget to—"
"Put it in the bin! I know, Mom!"

Elliot took out the trash,

brushed his teeth,

put on his pajamas,

crawled into bed,

but all he could think of was HarborFest.

"Did you remember to put the lid on the bin?"
"Yep!"
But . . . did he?

Elliot tried hard to sleep. He tossed, turned, and thought about corn-shucking contests and racing whaleboats and—

CLANG!
What was that? BANG! There it was again.

ELLIOT'S ADVENTURES

Elliot
and the Raccoons' Wild Party

BY INGRID SIMUNIC
illustrated by VIKTORIA SKAKANDI

DSCVR
KEEP DISCOVERING

Elliot went to investigate.

He tiptoed to the side door, opened it quietly, and peeked outside. Everything was quiet. Everything was still . . .

. . . until a metal bin lid came crashing out from behind the bins, trundled past him down the driveway, and finished with a thunderous roll and a noisy landing.

Elliot pointed his flashlight toward the bins.

Raccoons!
He must have forgotten the lids!

A wildlife expert who had visited Elliot's class said raccoons shouldn't be thought of as nuisances to eliminate but as wildlife to protect.

But what Elliot saw now sure looked like a nuisance!

He watched the plump little comedians feast on discarded pizza crusts and old cheese. One raccoon lifted a half-eaten slice of watermelon over his head with a cheer. Another raccoon shook her head and then used her nimble fingers to open a Ziploc bag full of old, soggy strawberries. They were having a great time!

A third raccoon noticed Elliot. He sniffed and chittered and edged nearer. Elliot stood very still so he wouldn't frighten him.

Suddenly, the curious raccoon turned to his mates. He chirped, chattered, and darted away. The others answered and ran after him, leaving Elliot with a great big mess.

Elliot couldn't resist giving chase. After all, he wasn't even sleepy!

Down along the bay, the raccoons and Elliot ran until they reached a sandy beach, where the raccoons wrestled and tumbled.

With a sniff and a chirp, one raccoon darted off to a nearby house.

Uh-oh! A cat dish had been left out, and the food bin beside it had been left open.

The wildlife expert had said that taking pet food indoors at night was an important part of protecting raccoons. When they cause trouble, frustrated residents leave traps out to catch them.

The other raccoons joined in and made a great big mess. They moved on, and Elliot decided to tidy up behind them. It was best for the owners not to know they had caused trouble!

Elliot dashed in the direction the raccoons had gone, past the old windmill, and down the main street. There! Under the bright red lights of the Sag Harbor cinema, the three little animals scurried along.

Elliot stopped in his tracks. A dumpster dive!

The mischief-makers feasted. What didn't they eat? They had surf and turf, spaghetti with pickles, swordfish à la coffee grounds, old spinach on ice-cream. What a buffet!

With one hand, Elliot pinched his nose. With the other, he picked up bits thrown from torn garbage bags while the raccoons chowed down.

Why, Elliot wondered, didn't the restaurants lock their bins at night? If food was within reach, who could blame the raccoons?

Satisfied at last, the full-bellied raccoons moved on—this time more slowly. Once the bins were safely shut, Elliot followed. Where had they gone?

Elliot kept an eye out for his new friends, but he was getting tired. If he didn't want to let the team down tomorrow, he needed to get some rest.

Elliot stood still to listen for the raccoons. Just when he thought he'd lost them, he heard a whimper.
Elliot jogged toward the sound, alongside a house, and past some garbage cans. The bins were strapped tight to keep the trash away from prying little paws. Clever, Elliot thought.

The cry grew louder.

Then he found them.

"Don't be scared," Elliot whispered. "Kit, can I call you that? Maybe I can get you out. And you, what do you have there? A marshmallow?"

Elliot's heart pounded. Was it dangerous to help? Would the raccoons get hurt? Would he? Oh, what had he been thinking when he chased after them? And why didn't he just close the bins up tight? He should be in bed!

No matter what, Elliot could not leave his friends behind. He studied the door.

"Ah ha!" With a pinch and a click, the trap door swung open, and the raccoons were free.

The three happy raccoons chattered and purred and ran circles around their hero.
Elliot had saved them!
"This was fun, guys, but I'd better get to bed."

Elliot ran home, and the raccoons followed.

"What a mess! I'll have some cleaning up to do tomorrow," Elliot said. "Well, goodnight. Try not to get in any more trouble!"

The raccoons chattered goodnight.

In the morning, Elliot woke up and marveled at his dream.

He served himself a bowl of cereal and sat down to eat.

Just then, he heard Mom gasp outside.
The bins!

Elliot ran to the side window and looked outside. The bins weren't closed tight, but everything was tidy. Of course, it had only been a dream. Hadn't it?

But then Mom said, "I found this on the doorstep. A half-eaten marshmallow?"

"A thank you, I think," Elliot said.

BONUS
Coloring Pages

Have a good time with

Elliot's coloring pages!

CPSIA information can be obtained
at www.ICGtesting.com
Printed in the USA
LVHW070144140921
697761LV00019B/604